Beyond the Shore

Beyond the Shore

Kenneth M. Krakaur

Bujew
Press

Dedication

To my wife, Priscilla, who puts up with my sailing obsession; the weekly day sailing on the James River, the annual cruising in the Caribbean, and the occasional sailing trips to New England on the Atlantic Ocean.

To my children, Rachel and Allison, who have shared many days sailing on *Last Call* and *Instant Karma*.

To Jade Peters, Cape Town, South Africa, who provided the inspiration for this book, and,

To those who have stepped beyond their shore to seek adventure on the high seas.

Note to the Reader

This book contains some technical sailing terms
which are explained in the glossary.

Chapter One

In the Beginning

New math, old math, algebra, history, geometry, trigonometry, geography, sociology, anthropology, foreign language, literature, creative writing, uncreative writing, geography, geography, geography, graduation. I was supposed to be thinking about what comes next, but I could not find a direction in my life. At age eighteen with more geography classes than I wish to describe I was led to believe that I must leave my land to explore what lies beyond.

My country shares its history with the likes of great countries, United States and Germany. We share the unfortunate acts of our ancestors. We share these unfortunate acts with other countries that have chosen to kill for political reasons, for social reasons. America killed the Native Americans, the Nazis killed the Jews and Christians and we killed Africans. My continent of Africa is a killing field. In my father's day, it was the Biafran War in Nigeria. That was a war of mass starvation. It occurred when my father was in his teens. The world mildly cared. Since then the world turned its eye away from mass genocide in Uganda, Somalia, Ethiopia, Sudan, Congo, and Sierra Leone. The world ignored two million killed in Cambodia. The white world, the one of which I am a part, does not really care about blacks or Asians. My guess is that if just 2,000 or 3,000 Brits or Yanks were killed in a terrorist act, the world would react quite differently.

Humans are killers; always have been, always will be. Sadly it's part of the human condition, it's what we are. We are followers of leaders. The leaders are killers. I am not and will never be part of the *we*. Growing up in Cape Town, I watched the world demonize us. At age eighteen, I didn't know what to feel about the world or its future.

For years, during study hall, I tried to understand why we are the way we are. I decided that all people act on the basis of four motivators. I could think of no act that falls outside these motivators, however, at age eighteen, I knew I hadn't thought of everything. The four motivators are love/sex, fear, greed, and hate. I think this discovery was more important than what I learned in 13 years of public education. Or maybe my public education pointed me to this realization.

My family is worth a brief discussion. My father is a middle-aged, balding executive. He is the son of an accountant, the grandson of a restaurant manager, and the great-grandson of a grocer, who came to Cape Town from Eastern Europe. My father is a nonpracticing Jew. My mother is a gemologist, the daughter of a New Zealand journalist, the granddaughter of a farmer, and the great-granddaughter of a Brit whose occupation is unknown. My mother is a non-practicing Catholic. My father is obsessed with retirement; my mother is obsessed with gems.

When my eldest brother was born, my mother, who really wanted a girl, named him Robert E. The "R" in Robert stood for ruby and the "E" for emerald. When the next child was born, he was named David S. The "D" in

David was for diamond, and the "S" for sapphire. When I was born, my mother ran out of precious stones. So she resorted to a stone of little significance, a stone associated with the Orient and little fat Buddhas. Don't call me Ishmael, call me Jade. No middle initial. No religion. She ran out of everything when I came along. Despite my diatribe on the naming convention of my family, my parents are loving, kind, and caring parents and people. Actually I would be happy if I turned out like either of them.

Robert and David would best be described as a dictionary definition of stability. At age eighteen, each left Cape Town to attend college in Great Britain. Both completed graduate studies in America. Robert received his MBA from the College of William and Mary, while David received his MBA from Stanford. Both returned to the U.K., two years apart, got big jobs in London, dated and married Brits, had one child each, neither following my family's naming convention, own homes outside London, and rarely travel back to Cape Town. My father is happy for them and their successes, while my mother is sad for the lack of contact she has with her grandchildren.

In the years following my high school graduation, my relationship with my brothers became strained. They never could understand why I was not following in their footsteps, and they did not respect me. And while they never said such, the message had been made in sarcastic one-liners, and the never ending comments about getting a purpose or a vision for the future. They saw London as the center of the universe. I did not. Business and London just did not appeal to me. Business was a part of the greed motivator and London was essential to that matrix.

Of the four motivators, the love motivator was what I was really in search of. And love itself takes on so many meanings. At age eighteen, I was not in search of love for someone but rather for something. I needed to make sure that the love for something did not turn into greed.

After graduation I spent several months working odd jobs for a temp agency; that was my job by day. At night I took classes at a local college in the culinary arts. After the stress of a day job and night school, I decided to give the culinary arts full attention. Two years later I completed my studies and received a diploma that would allow me to function as an assistant chef, somewhere between short order cook and chef.

At age twenty-one nothing had improved with my relationship with my brothers. My father was closing in on retirement and my mother was still collecting and selling gems. I was sick of working in hot kitchens under the supervision of over-educated, arrogant and abusive chefs and restaurant managers. The pay was also poor and job security was nonexistent. On the day of my twenty second birthday I sat alone in the restaurant where I was working. I had very few friends, no boyfriend, had not been dating, and had not fallen in love with anything.

By the time midnight arrived I had consumed two martinis and was totally absorbed by the "want ads." Then I saw it. This was the ad that could bring together geography, instability, and the culinary arts. It was the first time in such a long time that I heard myself say, "This is something I would really love to do." The ad read:

> *Wanted: Experienced cook to join delivery crew. Sailing in 30 days (Cape Town to the Caribbean). Contact John at Mac Delivery Service, Cape Town.*

Chapter Two

A Turn of Events

On my twenty-second birthday plus one day, I contacted Mac Delivery Service and spoke to John. John arranged delivery of sailing vessels manufactured in South Africa for the charter trade, worldwide. The vessel to be delivered was a Bluewater 46 catamaran. The charter company was Bluewater Cat Charters, one of the largest charter companies on the globe. The vessel was built by Hamilton and Huffman of Cape Town. The vessel was designed by naval architect David Bridges, also of Cape Town. The combination of Hamilton and Huffman and Bridges was big in the catamaran business and now rivaled the various

French catamaran designer/builders who had cornered the cat trade just a decade earlier.

My phone call with John was a blend of small-talk and business; no different than any two people seeking to make a deal. John was a professional who had a lot of practice judging crew for his delivery business. The initial phone call quickly became a phone interview. The main issues to be sorted out centered around the basics; criminal record, experience, availability, and commitment. I was clean on the criminal record, availability and commitment but very dirty on experience. At the end of the phone call, John suggested that I come over to the office for a formal interview. We agreed to meet the next day. I was very nervous about my upcoming personal meeting. Sunrise occurred at 7 a.m. and by 8 a.m., I was on my way to see John.

He ran me through a multi-staged interview process. I failed to answer most of the questions correctly. I knew nothing about sailing, nothing about the sea, and nothing about what may lie ahead of me if I was selected for the assignment. After a few hours with John, and a lot of unanswered questions, he told me that he would like for me to talk to the other crew, Patrick and Phil. Patrick and Phil had delivered many vessels before, sometimes together and sometimes with other crew. They were seasoned sailors and the confidence John had in them was large and very obvious. I thanked John for the consideration and said I would wait for his call. The following day brought no response from Mac Delivery Service. The following week brought no response. I told no one about my prospect as I thought landing an assignment like this was a long shot.

On the ninth day following my visit to Mac Delivery Service I got a call from John asking me to come to the office to meet with Patrick, Phil, and him. On day ten we met, we talked, they interrogated me about my cooking skills, my sailing skills, and my ability to spend two months at sea with two men ages twenty-nine and thirty. Both men were married and I hoped that they were interested in remaining faithful to their wives. In the final half-hour of our meeting I thought we had a breakthrough as the discussion shifted to departure dates, provisions, salary, etc.

On day eleven, John called to congratulate me on my new assignment, my new life, and perhaps my new love. The next real issue to overcome was telling my parents about my new adventure. As I said earlier, my family is rooted in stability; adventure is a foreign concept. I needed to move the process along as my departure was set for January 31, 2000, just two weeks away. I also had to quit my job, buy some sailing gear, sublet my room, and tie up several other loose ends in my life. There were no real friends to say goodbye to and no boyfriend to leave behind. Up until now my life had been so dull, so stable, and so predictable. It was time to say goodbye to my shore and to say goodbye to Cape Town. At age twenty-two my life was to take a turn and I hoped it was a turn for the best.

The next evening I called my mother and told her I would be over for breakfast. In the restaurant business evenings are never yours. She seemed concerned but curious. I knew my father would be very much against this and I needed my mother's support. Her full support was unlikely. The drive over was nerve-racking. I was anticipating anger, tears, lack of support, and my mother begging or perhaps insisting that I not go. This is how stable people react to adventure.

The smell of breakfast was nonexistent. The atmosphere was cold. I was thankful that my father was not home. Work starts early for him. The coffee was brewing and the table was set for two. My mother greeted me with a sad smile. We walked to the kitchen table and sat down. My mother wore her favorite ring, a ring she inherited from her grandmother, and the ring that my mother said began her interest in gems. Then she asked me in her South African-New Zealand voice, "Jade, what's wrong? You look like you have bad news to tell me."

"Mother, it's time for me to go, to leave Cape Town, to leave South Africa." With that, tears began to fall from her eyes. There was no anger, no other emotion. She just stared into her coffee. The black coffee reflected onto her face. She looked strange to me.

"Where will you go, what will you do?" I told her about Mac Delivery Service, Patrick and Phil, and the pending departure date. Her only reply was to say that Kiwi blood runs deep through my veins. She told me that when she was a young girl, she read a book by Hermann Hesse called *Siddhartha*. The book tells the story of a young man who becomes a priest and leaves his family, much to the disappointment of his father. In the end the father realizes that every child, every person, must find their own way in the world.

"Jade, that is why when Robert and David left for the U.K. they found no resistance from me. You, like them, must find your own path to happiness. If it is not here, then search beyond this shore."

The question of how to break the news to my father became the focal point. My mother said that there was no good way other than head-on. She guessed my father would try to talk me out of it. There's that weird bond between dads and daughters and mothers and sons. I asked my mother to talk to him first. She thought that was a bad idea.

"Jade, you must tell him. He'll understand."

"I don't think so," I thought to myself.

So at noon, I drove to his office hoping I could catch him for lunch. At 12:30, I walked into his office to ask him if I could join him for a quick bite to eat. He was surprised to see me. It was unusual for me to show up unplanned.

"So, to what do I owe this honor?"

"Dad, we need to talk."

"Okay, over lunch?"

"Sure."

We walked to Dell's Tavern, ordered two iced teas and two Caesar salads.

"So, what do you want to talk about?" he asked.

I launched into my plans. He was stunned, shocked, and sad.

"Why do you have to do this? Please reconsider. Who is Mac Delivery Service? Who are Patrick and Phil? What do you know about sailing?"

"Dad, I have to do this. I have to find my way in the world. I have Kiwi blood in my veins."

"I see you have already talked to your mother."

He had heard this twice before from Robert and David. He was realizing that all his children would be adrift and wondered why none of them chose to stay in Cape Town. Was it he and my mother who chased us away from South Africa?

"I know you won't listen to me. You've always been your own person. You've never liked stability. Go do this if you must, but please don't forget me." A tear rolled down his cheek and then six rolled down mine. We stood up, hugged, and departed. I walked to my car, got in, closed the door, and sobbed. The decision was made and approved. My life was about to change in a major way.

Chapter Three

The Ghost

The Saturday night following the meeting with my parents was my last day as a land-based assistant chef. Business was unusually slow at Smyth's Bistro, so I said my goodbyes and was out of the restaurant by 10:30 p.m. On my way back to my room I decided to stop by Reubens, one of the most upscale restaurants in Cape Town. I always wanted to go there but never had.

"One drink at the bar to celebrate my departure from Smyth's and then back on the road," I thought.

That was the plan, clean and simple. Things just didn't turn out that way.

When I arrived at Reubens, the bar was empty. I took a seat near the middle and lit up a cigarette, expecting it to be the last. I ordered a martini, dry and dirty, and on the rocks. I was in an odd talkative mood so I scanned the bar for a friendly face. Down at one end of the bar was a man who looked to be close to forty, drinking what I had just ordered, and reading a sailing magazine. When my drink came, I picked it up and walked to where he was sitting and introduced myself.

"Excuse me. I noticed you are reading a sailing magazine. Are you a sailor?" He swiveled his chair around in my direction and looked at me expecting to see someone older. He was tall, thin, and had a warm and honest smile. I looked into his eyes. One was blue and one was brown. I had never seen anyone like that before.

"Yes, I sail on the Chesapeake Bay."

"Where's that?" I asked.

"In the U.S., East Coast, near Washington, D.C."

Then he extended his hand and said, "Michael Kenney."

"How do you do, Mr. Kenney."

"Call me Michael."

"Very well, Michael."

"And your name?"

"Jade."

"Jade, nice to meet you." He reminded me of what my father may have been like twenty years earlier before the years of work stress corrupted his physical well-being.

"So Jade, thinking of buying a boat?"

"No sir, but I'm about to crew on a Blue-water 46."

"Nice boat."

Then I went on to tell him the whole story surrounding my impending trip. He listened very attentively. We both had another drink and then I asked, "Well, do you have any advice for me, Michael?"

He took out his billfold and withdrew a small plastic packet, matchbook size. "Jade, I want you to have this. It is filled with colored sand. This sand was given to me by Paul Curry, a dear friend of mine, back in the states. This sand comes from a Buddhist mandala, a sand painting. It has spiritual significance. It speaks of life's impermanence. The Tibetan monks who created this mandala, did so as part of a prayer ritual. The mandala is beautiful, and the effort that goes into its creation is immense. Shortly after the mandala is completed, it is destroyed. This is done to illustrate life's impermanence and to recognize that death is a part of life. They believe in reincarnation, as I do. You must carry it with you for the rest of your life. The sand will guide you.

"Jade, there are thirteen things you must remember. I will assume that your Judeo-Christian upbringing gave you ten; the sand will guide you to two of them. I will give you one. The first ten are the Ten Commandments. Modernize them as you wish. Numbers eleven and twelve come from the sand. You are in search of a new beginning. You are in search of inner peace. Inner peace can only come from the convergence of wisdom and compassion. When you don't know what to do, place the sand in your hand and remember: be wise, make your decisions carefully, use logic, not emotion. Be compassionate, think about others, make sure you understand how your decisions will affect others, look for the best in others and seek to understand before you seek to be understood. And number thirteen, I call the Platinum Rule. Do onto others as they would want done to themselves. Do not presuppose you know what is right for someone else. Godspeed, Jade."

I glanced down into my drink. The drink was empty. I looked up to Michael. He was gone. He vanished like a ghost in a dream. The only difference was the sand packet that lay in my hand as evidence that my ghost was real.

That night I went to my room and logged on to the Internet. Michael could not have known that I was totally out of touch with religion. I searched the Ten Commandments. There were many versions and interpretations. When all was said and done I had my thirteen principles.

1. *I will find a belief in a god*
2. *He will be my only god*
3. *I will not use his name in vain*
4. *I will designate time for prayer*
5. *I will honor my parents*
6. *I will not harm anyone or anything*
7. *I will not commit adultery*
8. *I will not steal*
9. *I will not lie*
10. *I will not be ruled by my desires*
11. *I will always make careful decisions*
12. *I will be compassionate, caring and kind*
13. *I will treat others as they wish to be treated*

Chapter Four

Renovatio

On January twenty-fifth, I met my father at Raleigh Marine, the premier bluewater outfitter in Cape Town. Seventeen hundred dollars later, less than either of my brother's educational costs, net of mine, I was outfitted with foul weather gear, tether, harness, strobe light, knife and other assorted safety gear. I also purchased several charts, a handheld GPS (Global Positioning System), a personal EPIRB (Emergency Position Indicating Radio Beacon), *The Seamanship and Survival Manual* authored by Magoon & Associates, and a *Cooking At Sea Guide* by L. A. Donahue. Both authors were from the Chesapeake Bay region. I wondered if either of them knew Michael Kenney.

By January twenty-ninth, all loose ends were tightened up. No more chef job, car sold, room sublet, goodbyes made to friends, goodbyes made to Robert and David, but the final goodbye to my parents was hanging over my head. The thought of more tears and hugs gave me a nervous stomach.

On January thirtieth, I met Phil and Patrick at Mac Delivery Service. The boat had been provisioned by John and my gear loaded on a brand new Bluewater 46 cat. Her name was *Renovatio*. I asked Phil and Patrick what *Renovatio* meant and they said they didn't know, only that the boat was owned by an Italian physician living in the U.S. Curious about the name, I went into John's office to use his computer, to search for the meaning of *Renovatio*. The Internet search revealed that *Renovatio* was Latin for renewal or re-birth. How fitting, I thought.

She was a beautiful vessel with four cabins, each with its own head. The galley was small but very functional with a four-burner propane stove and oven, double sinks and a refrigerator/freezer powered by a massive ice plate. The wood in the saloon was cherry and the general workmanship was excellent. The navigation station was equipped with VHF radio and GPS and other assorted navigation and safety gear. There were two life canisters on board. Each canister held a four-man, fully enclosed life raft. One was secured to the deck just behind the mast and the other was stored under one of the cockpit seats.

That night I lay in my bunk thinking of my blue-eyed, brown-eyed ghost. The only thing standing between me and my adventure was the farewell to my parents. As I lay there I thought about the thirteen things to remember. Ten from Moses, two from Buddha and one from Michael Kenney. I remembered my four motivators. I was in search of love. I tried to think of a nickname for the thirteen principles. They were Jewish. They were Buddhist. They were Buddhist. They were Jewish. The thirteen principles of Bujew, I thought, and I had the sand to prove it. I fell asleep at 4:00 a.m.

The day that followed my sleepless night was one of those days that I will remember for the rest of my life. By 7:30 a.m. I was up and showered. My long light brown hair was braided. My father always liked my hair that way. I tried to look my best, but after a nearly sleepless night, my best was slightly better than poor. I stared into the mirror. I was shocked how tired and worn-out I looked. At 8 a.m. my parents arrived at Mac Delivery Service. I greeted them and walked down to *Renovatio*.

"Good morning, Dad," kissing him on the cheek.

"Good morning, honey," he replied. "Well, I guess I can't talk you out of this."

"No, I have to do this. I am a Kiwi."

"Yes, your mother reminded me of that on the drive over." Silence fell over us.

"How about a tour of my quarters?" I asked, trying to change the mood of our discussion.

"Sure," he replied. The three of us walked below and began our quick tour.

"Jade, this boat is so small."

"Not really, Dad." More silence. Then thankfully Patrick and Phil arrived with the final checklist of equipment and provisions. I introduced my parents to them. That went well. Then Patrick indicated we'd be leaving in thirty minutes or so. For the next twenty minutes, the three of us sat in my cabin reviewing my itinerary. My father wanted details about dates and times, but the best I could do was to offer generalities. He said very little and made no eye contact.

We walked back to the car, my father leading the way. His composure was failing. My composure was failing. He turned to look at me and we both fell apart. Nothing else could be said. My mother kissed me and walked away. My father and I hugged. I said nothing. We sobbed, we separated and I quickly walked back to *Renovatio*. Phil and Patrick were back in the office. I sat on the edge of my bed and cried. My father was really hurting and I knew I was responsible for that pain. I grabbed the sand. Talk to me Michael Kenney, talk to me. Then I heard a voice, "Jade, we need to shove off." I came topside.

Phil and Patrick smiled. "Are you okay?"

"Yes, I'll be fine." I took a deep breath.

"Your dad is really struggling, isn't he?" asked Patrick.

"Yes he is. I feel so responsible. It's killing him."

"We go through this with our wives. It happens every time."

"Are my parents gone?" I said while choking up.

"Yes, they're gone."

I put the sand in my pocket. "Thanks, Michael," I thought to myself. *Renovatio*, re-birth, Bujew, inner peace.

I tossed the bow lines as the two diesel engines moved us toward the harbor. Then Patrick called, "Jade, what's for lunch?" It was 9:00 a.m. We smiled at each other. "Don't worry, things will be okay." The tone in his voice was like that of an older brother talking to his kid sister.

"I hope so. I hope you didn't make a mistake hiring me on as crew."

"Trust me, you'll be fine." He smiled and shot me a wink.

I went below and retrieved my seamanship manual. I was halfway through reading the book and my general understanding about sailing and seamanship was weak but improving. I was very concerned about my first watch. Watch is all about watching: watching instruments, compass, and all things around you. Patrick had given me a crash course on what I had to do while on watch. Every half-hour I was to record various data, like wind speed, boat speed, course, weather observations, etc. The data was recorded in the ship's logbook. I also had to check the autopilot settings and the GPS. From the GPS, I would record the boat's position. The guys would plot the long and lat on the charts on their watch. I was not quite ready for that.

Chapter Five

The Journey Begins

Day one at sea could best be described as a bowl of potpourri, a mixture of things all with a common scent. Our course was set for Salvador, Brazil. The distance to our destination was 3,334 nautical miles; our expected days at sea, twenty-one. The stop in Brazil was all for the purpose of taking on provisions, fuel and maintenance. It would also give Phil an opportunity to check in with John back at Mac. There was no time for parental or spousal visitation. We had a schedule to keep and in this business time is money. Some deliveries are paid per diem. Our contract was per delivery. The longer it took to deliver, the lower our per diem. I had no idea how much Patrick and Phil were receiving in compensation. My pay would equate to forty dollars per day if we maintained our schedule; not a lot of money but a lot of adventure. Who needs money, anyway? I basically had no living expenses, no debt, and no smoking habit. I left the smoking habit back in Cape Town. Best of all, I had a future and a direction and a small packet of sand.

The watch schedule was posted on the galley wall. It covered the expected duration of the trip. It was generated by some computer program that gave the cook less watch than the others. It did require me to respond to any "all hands on deck" call, day or night.

Patrick's and Phil's expectations at meal time were far less than the customers at Smyth's Bistro and my inventory of spices and condiments was sparse, anyway. Cooking would be easy, as long as the sea was kind.

Clearing the harbor and moving into open waters only took an hour. As I looked out at the vastness and emptiness in front of me, I felt a slight panicky feeling come on. Then I reached into my pocket and felt the packet of sand. Things settled down inside of me. The first morning and afternoon was a textbook sail, according to my crew members. My cooking duties went well as far as I could tell. Dinner was another matter. The seas were up and *Renovatio* surfed down large swells generated by southeast winds. The stove was gimbaled which helped. I was not. I needed to find my sea legs. I did get the job done and Patrick and Phil said the dinner was perfect. I think they had low expectations.

By 9:15 p.m., I was so seasick. The frequency of vomiting was alarming, and the Bonine I had taken was doing nothing. Phil was asleep in his cabin unaffected by the sea. Patrick, the more brotherly and sensitive one, was at the helm. The autopilot was engaged and doing its job. "How's the chef doing?" Patrick yelled over the sound of the sea.

"Not so good."

"Hang in there. It happens to everyone. Stay hydrated. That's the most important thing."

By 11:00 p.m. I was asleep and dreaming. Dreams are funny things. Your mind reassembles facts, often creating nonsense but other times creating visions. Tonight was a cross between "Alice in Wonderland" and "The Wizard of Oz." I sat in the lap of a ten-foot Jade Buddha. The Buddha was talking to me. The voice was Michael's. "Go for adventure. With adventure you'll be challenged; don't give up your dream. Don't give up your dream. Don't give up your dream." I woke up at 5:30 a.m., very groggy.

"I am Jade; no address, no country, no ground under my feet, only a passport that says where I was from and nothing to say where I was going. Is this freedom or prison," I wondered.

Sunrises are more spectacular than sunsets. Sunsets last longer; sunrises, while shorter, illuminate more sky. Today's sunrise was as beautiful as I've ever seen. The sky was on fire with so many shades of red and orange. I needed to take advantage of this, as many sunrises would bring gray skies, rain, and howling winds. But not today; this was made for me. This was a gift. I smiled to myself. So many colors like the sand. Days two and three were beautiful days at sea. Steady winds from the southeast created six to eight foot fat rolling swells. *Renovatio* took advantage of the swells, accelerating down each and every one. Average speed was ten knots. Each day we ran the engines in order to keep the batteries topped off and the cold plate frozen. Our refrigerator-freezer was really working well and I was confident that the perishable items would keep until consumed.

Most notable was how Phil was warming up. Phil is the planner, he is the logician, chief navigator. Phil would rather do this type of work than man the helm. Phil tolerates watch; it's just part of his job. Patrick on the other hand loves the helm and loves watch. That said, we had yet to sail without the use of the autopilot.

In the past seventy-two hours, I had seen nature at its best, dreaming good things at night, developing friendships with Phil and Patrick and had not needed to hold the sand. I did miss my parents. I wished I could tell them how happy I was and that I was okay. That would have to wait until our first landfall, now eighteen days and 2,800 miles away.

The next morning I awoke to cloudy skies and light rain. The wind remained unchanged. A low pressure system was awaiting us, and Phil, also our weather expert, was preparing for declining conditions. He suggested that I shower now rather than later. Undressed in the very small head, I looked at myself. Three days at sea had made a difference; three days of not smoking was surely helping. I had no withdrawal symptoms. My arms looked trimmer and stronger and my face was nicely tanned. Everything about me looked better. I smiled at myself in the mirror and the reflection smiled back. Life was good, at least for now.

My morning watch greeted me with clouds, cool temperatures and drizzly conditions. Both Patrick and Phil were resting down below. The engines had done their work. All systems have been topped off. It was time to take a risk. I set the autopilot to standby mode. The helm was now in my hands. "Keep *Renovatio* on course. God, I have butterflies. It feels good to be out of my comfort zone," I thought. The winds made a slight shift. The sails luffed. I leaned toward the winch and trimmed the sails, one hand on the wheel, one hand on the winch. The luff disappeared. "I am the helmsman, I am the captain. Autopilot, who needs the autopilot?"

"Wisdom, Jade, wisdom," I heard in my head. "Take it slow and steady."

Chapter Six

All Hands On Deck

The sky ahead looked dark. It looked evil. I re-engaged the autopilot and started to mentally prepare for bad weather. Then I heard a noise from within the cabin. Patrick and Phil emerged. "Jade, prepare the galley for rough conditions. Secure everything you can. Take a Bonine. The barometer is falling fast and the six-hour trend looks bad. We are in for a rough ride. Put on a life jacket." A knot grew in my stomach. The galley needed little attention. I put away the morning dishes and secured a few items that were not fully secured. I popped a Bonine. I took out my lightweight foul weather gear, tightened the belt on my shorts, (my waistline was shrinking), and slipped into my life jacket, harness and tether. I was scared to death. "Be brave," I thought to myself.

Within an hour we were in the thick of the storm. *Renovatio* was now climbing larger swells as the wind shifted around to the north. Phil and Patrick reefed the jib and the mainsail as I sat in the cockpit watching the autopilot do its thing. Phil commented that if the winds picked up over forty knots that we would have to manually steer and not overtax the autopilot mechanism. I remained scared but also confident in Phil and Patrick. I was less confident in myself. The winds now exceeded forty knots and we put another reef in the mainsail. *Renovatio* continued to climb and bang. We decided to fall off to ease the pounding. The course change would not affect us very much. For six hours we struggled on.

I was now on vomit number twelve, however, I had been vomit-free for a little over an hour. As we moved away from the edge of the low pressure area, the winds and the seas calmed and the autopilot went on temporarily. Then I hit the standby mode.

"Patrick, help me. I need to learn how to

steer in tougher conditions."

"Sure, move over, Sis." We shared the seat at the helm and he coached me through the swells.

"That's it . . . don't oversteer. Easy does it. You're doing great."

"Thanks, Patrick."

"No problem, Sis." He patted me on the back and went below to use the head.

Phil glanced over. "Nice job during the storm."

"Thanks, Phil." Wow, a compliment from Phil.

"Jade, how about a fresh pot of coffee?"

"Sure." I turned the helm over to Phil and went below. Things continued to settle down and by evening we were fed, tired, and best of all, the low pressure had moved out to the east and smooth sailing was ahead of us.

Nothing particularly noteworthy happened during the next few days other than we continued to compile miles at sea. There was more time in the galley, more time at the helm, more time on watch, and more time in the rack. Phil continued to warm up; he now called me Sis. It felt great to be sailing with my new brothers.

My dreams had been good. My brain was

assembling things correctly now. I dreamt of my childhood, and great times with my parents. My older brothers Diamond and Ruby did not appear in any of my dreams. I dreamt of Tim, a boy who lived on my street when I was in elementary school. Tim was the boy I thought I would marry when I saw the world though my eyes at age eleven. I hadn't seen Tim since fifth grade. He moved to Nice, France, when his dad was transferred with his job.

My biggest problem was that my pants no longer fit. I couldn't put any more holes in my belt, so I had to resort to a piece of rope woven through my belt loops. Each day my health improved, no smoking, no snacking, three square meals a day, salt air and good dreams. We had traveled 1,344 miles so far. In two more days we would cross the midway point on our journey to South America.

Chapter Seven

Scarred for Life

On our tenth day at sea, we crossed the middle of our first leg of the trip. The last two days had brought more good weather, great sunrises and sunsets, good food, and great learning. I had completed the reading of my survival manual, as well as my sailing skills book provided to me by Phil. I had worn out two yellow highlighters, and my command of the sailing language was beginning to rival my brothers. I had ignored my cooking manual so far. Phil and Patrick were happy with my cooking skills.

On day eleven we began to experience a change in the weather. It was likely to be a terrible day at sea. The waves grew to fifteen feet and the wind gusted to forty-five knots. We were back in our life jackets, foul weather gear, tethers and harness. All hands were on deck. I stared out from the stern, both hands holding onto anything that would assist me in staying in one place. Staring out from the stern only reinforced my comfort with the past. The immediate future looked terrifying. We had little information regarding the weather patterns that we were about to face and I feared that we would be in this mess for a long time.

A crash sounded from the galley. "Jade, take a look." I could not tell whose voice it was as it could not compete with the loudness created by the howling wind. Things in the galley looked dreadful. Two cabinet locks had shattered and all the pots and pans were now on the galley floor. From my cabin I retrieved a duffel bag and began to place all the galleyware inside. Then another crash occurred, as the hull pounded through the surf. The crash sent the one remaining pot, not yet placed in the bag, into my chin. The pain was immediate and severe. There was a steady stream of bright red blood flowing down my neck. "Don't panic," I said to myself. Nearby a dishtowel lay on the floor. "Pressure will stop the bleeding," I thought. I had highlighted that section in my book. "Apply pressure."

Renovatio continued to crash through the waves. My concern about the bleeding and the racing of my heart left no room for panic. "Sis, are you okay in there?" Phil had stuck his head into the galley. Before I could answer, he said, "Damn, what happened? Patrick, we have a problem. Try and hold her steady." Phil tended to my chin. He applied surgical strips and a large piece of surgical tape. "Come on Jade, get on your feet, we need you in the cockpit. We are going to reef again." I reached into my pocket, no sand. I reached into the other pocket, no sand. Looked right. Looked left. Nothing. Then Phil extended his hand, the sand. "Here. Now let's go."

Things in the cockpit looked no better than they did in the galley. The hard bimini kept us fairly dry but the layers of salt on the cockpit window made it difficult to see. The raindrops stung my face. My chin had become numb, and I wondered how large the laceration on my chin was. The scar, which I would carry for the rest of my life, would be a reminder of my adventure, and my escape from Cape Town.

For hour upon hour we continued on. *Renovatio* was holding her own. Phil and Patrick seemed to have things under control. "When is this going to end?" I thought.

Despite the insanity, the guys were hungry and thirsty. "Jade, can you get us something, anything."

"Sure."

"Let's stay hydrated," one of them said. I retrieved six packs of cheese and crackers, two for each and three bottles of water. They were consumed in minutes. "Jade, go down below and get some rest. We will wake you if and when we need you." I wondered why they thought I could sleep under these conditions. I stored my wet foul weather gear in the head. I would normally have stripped down to my underwear but I was too scared. "Jade, remember to be wise, make good decisions." I could hear Michael's voice in my head.

I decided to sleep in my clothes with my life jacket on, and with my tether clipped to the outside of my harness. I began to feel seasick. I closed my eyes and fell asleep. Sleep lasted just a few minutes as I was thrown about my bunk. My chin momentarily collided with my fists. The pain was surreal. I dozed off again. Nightmare. I was at my father's funeral. I forced myself awake. I dozed off again. *Renovatio* was taking on water and sinking. I forced myself awake again. Nightmare after nightmare continued and my needed rest was not achieved. Finally I woke to Patrick's gentle tapping on my arm. "Sis, you've been down for three hours. Can you take watch with Phil? I need to catch a few winks."

"Give me five minutes. I'll be right up."

"Thanks."

Phil seemed undeterred by the circumstances. He steered *Renovatio* through the surf. I really admired his skill and looked up to him. I appreciated his seriousness, preparation and the caring attitude he had for each of us. How fortunate I was to be on a crew with these two guys. Two hours later, Patrick replaced Phil in the cockpit. Darkness was moving in and I dreaded the next twelve hours. Then Phil appeared back in the cockpit. His expression showed uneasiness.

"What's wrong, Phil?" Patrick and I said in unison.

"Something is leaking. The bilge is full and the pump is not keeping up. Jade, it's all yours. Keep us safe." Phil and Patrick vanished. The stress I was feeling was indescribable. I wanted to cry but I could not allow myself to be weak. They needed me and I needed them.

Despite the falling temperatures, my hands sweated, as I steered *Renovatio* through the darkness. "Prevent the hulls from getting buried. Watch for rogue waves. Hold the course. Don't oversteer." All those thoughts were running through my head. Then Phil emerged. "We found the problem. The water intake hose for the starboard engine has a serious leak. We are down to one engine for now. Start the port engine and put her in gear. We will need to top off the batteries."

"Done," I replied.

"By the way, the bilge pump is working now. I'll fill you in later."

"Right."

For the next two hours I sat in the cockpit, tethered in and alone. Steering for hours in rough seas was exhausting and I needed rest desperately. Phil emerged again. "Starboard engine repaired. We are back to two engines. By the way, I got a weather report from another vessel. We will be out of this mess in no time." By 11:00 p.m. the winds relaxed to fifteen knots and Phil and Patrick took over. I retreated to my galley responsibilities and prepared a light dinner.

Later that evening I finally had the opportunity to get some shut-eye. As I started to fall asleep, I could feel a pulse in my chin. I still was unable to determine the extent of the laceration, but as I said before, the scar was something that I hoped would never fade away. I thought about how I would respond to people when they asked me how I got the scar. I think I would simply say, "I got it at sea."

Chapter Eight

Salvador

The days following the storm were good days. We had the chance to talk to several ships we could see on the horizon and all indications were that we would be in a favorable weather pattern for the next week. We still had 1,482 miles to go before landfall in Salvador, Brazil. At our average speed of seven knots it would take approximately nine days for us to reach our destination.

Each day that drifted by seemed to get better. The scar, my reminder of my adventure, looked to be about two centimeters long. Phil's medical care was good. The scar would be thin. I hoped it wouldn't fade away entirely. Like the name *Renovatio*, I had been reborn. I was no longer Jade of Cape Town. I was Jade of the sea. Each day my view of the world changed. I had two brothers now, who were adventurers like me. They had found a spot in my heart where David and Robert once resided. I knew they would be there forever, as Robert and David have been replaced.

Patrick and Phil had been talking about their wives. Susan and Donna would have like their husbands to stop delivering boats. They both wanted families and husbands who appreciated stability. Patrick and Phil also wanted children and were beginning to reconcile the need to be home, if and when the decision was made to pursue a family. John from Mac Delivery Service used to make deliveries but stopped for the same reason described. Phil and Patrick needed to deal with this issue. At my age I could offer little advice on the matter.

Phil continued to be spooked by the failure of the engine hose and was committed to daily inspections of every thru-hull fitting, clamp, and hose on *Renovatio*. Each day he inspected and re-inspected, tightened clamps and entered into the logbook each and every problem encountered. The problems seemed to be isolated to plumbing. The electrical, refrigeration, rigging, and steering systems seemed to be okay for now. Patrick, however, was worried about the autopilot system, as he felt it was undersized for a 46-foot charter boat. Time would tell.

On my last watch I did a lot of thinking. I couldn't believe I ever smoked, or that I had let my physical condition be less than optimal. All my clothes were loose and I guessed I was down two or three dress sizes. Each day as I stripped in front of the mirror I was seeing a new me. I was strong and my stamina was remarkable. I had muscles. I made bodybuilder poses in front of the mirror and giggled inside. I wondered if I could maintain this level of fitness on shore.

By day seventeen, Phil's obsession with *Renovatio* had subsided. Patrick commented on how great I looked and said that I would need to watch out for the South American men. "Beat them away with a stick if you have to," he joked. That would be a change. Attracting the opposite sex had never been my strength. But I was a new Jade. Truth be known, the only man I really wanted to see was my father. I wanted him to see the new me, Jade the adventurer, the girl with Kiwi blood in her veins.

On day nineteen we arrived in Salvador, Brazil, at 9:00 a.m., local time. The arrival was bittersweet. It was great to have dirt under my feet but I was concerned about starting over again, and leaving land behind. Our immediate chore was to clear customs and then to get to the business of re-provisioning, minor repairs, phone calls home and buying some new clothes. We met for lunch at the Marina Grill. Phil had big news. Things were about to change. "Guys, we have a lot to talk about," Phil said. He looked different to me, more animated, like a little kid on Christmas morning. "First, I spoke to John. We need to delay the delivery by one week. There is a problem with the new owner. John said it had something to do with the owner's bank loan and the import tariff. He's going to give us six days off with a food per diem of twenty-five dollars per-day, per-crew member. Or if we want, we can continue on and take six days in the British Virgin Islands (BVIs) when we arrive. Our choice, but don't answer yet. I have other news."

"What, Phil?"

"Okay, Susan's pregnant and I may need to go home." Congratulations rang out from

Patrick.

"Congratulations, Papa," I smiled. "Well, I get to be an aunt again." I gave him a kiss on the cheek and his eyes welled up.

"Patrick, any news from home?" Phil asked.

"No, no big news, everything is okay with Donna."

"I'll let you know tomorrow what I'll be doing. I need to talk to John."

"Phil, if my opinion counts, let's take six days now. I would love to see if my parents could fly in for a few days."

"Okay with me. Patrick, any feelings on the issue?"

"I'm ready for a break and quite frankly, I've seen enough of the BVIs."

"Okay, let's plan on staying here. I'll let John know and I'll call Susan." With the decision made, I jogged to the phone booth.

Chapter Nine

Retirement Delayed

I had put off calling home, as I was afraid to hear my dad's voice. It was Saturday and I expected that someone would be home. The phone rang once and was picked up immediately. A thought flashed through my head. "Every call to my home from anyone was answered with the anticipation that it was me." I was putting them through hell. "Michael, where was my compassion?" I thought.

My father answered. My heart was beating hard. My butterflies flew. He answered the phone with my name.

"Jade?"

"Yes Dad, it's me."

"Is everything okay? Where are you?"

"Everything is fine. We are in Salvador, Brazil. "How's Mom?"

"She's fine. We have been thinking about you every minute of every day."

"Dad, this has been one of the greatest experiences of my life. But there's one thing that could make it even better. And that is to see you and Mom. I have six days off. Do you think you can fly to Salvador? I know it's a lot to ask."

"I'm already packing."

"Put Mom on the phone."

"I'm already on. How's my little gem, how's my little Kiwi?"

"Mom, I've learned so much so fast. The guys have adopted me as their kid sister and Susan's pregnant."

"Who is Susan?"

"Phil's wife. I don't know what that means for our trip but I will know by the end of the day."

"Jade, how can I get in contact with you?" my father asked.

"Call the marina. We are docked next to the office." I gave him the telephone number.

"I'll call you within an hour."

"Mom and Dad, I'm so excited. Wait until

you see me."

Forty-five minutes later the phone rang in the marina office. Karl, the marina office attendant, answered the phone and signaled to me. I took the phone. "Jade, great news. We have flights for tomorrow."

"Dad, this must be costing you a fortune. "

"Not to worry. I'll just delay retirement another month." We smiled at each other through the phone. He used that line so many times before. I said goodbye and ran to the boat.

"Patrick, Phil, my parents are flying in tomorrow." They stood up and gave me a big hug.

"Say, let's go into town. You need a new outfit. You can't see your parents in those clothes; you look like a starving child." The taxi ride into town took ten minutes and then shopping began: new shorts, new top, new belt and a haircut. I even bought some makeup. I never wore makeup, however, this was such a special occasion.

On Sunday I continued to work on my provisioning responsibilities. After the order was placed for the provisions I retreated to the marina shower to get ready for the visit of a lifetime. The water pressure and temperature were perfect. I closed my eyes and let the water cascade over my newly cut hair. I made believe I was being filmed for a shampoo commercial, that's how confident I felt about the new me. My new sleeveless cotton blouse revealed my new muscles; my new shorts revealed my toned legs. I added the makeup and looked deep into the mirror. Who was this woman? Who was this beautiful woman staring back at me? "Michael, if you could see me now." I kissed the packet of sand and placed it in my pocket. "Thanks, Mr. Kenney," I said out loud.

At 4:30 p.m. I sat on the bow of *Renovatio* waiting for my parents. Once again, butterflies filled my stomach. Then I heard a car door open and shut. The taxi pulled away and my parents emerged at the end of the pier. They took a quick look around and walked toward me. They got closer and closer. We made eye contact and I got ready to burst into joy, but they walked right past me. They didn't recognize me. Had I changed that much? Who was I? Who had I turned into, that my parents couldn't recognize their only daughter? "Mom, Dad." They both spun around, recognizing my voice. I leapt into their arms. We hugged for a long time, then we separated.

"Jade, my god, you look like a movie star."

"Like a shampoo commercial?" They looked at me with a questioning expression. We laughed and laughed. We walked to the marina's lounge where it was air-conditioned and sat down facing each other. "Jade, I want to hear everything but first I have something for you." My dad handed me an envelope, likely holding a greeting card. I opened it. The card was an "I Miss You" card from Robert and David. A folded piece of paper fell onto my lap.

Chapter Ten

The Reconciliation

Dear Jade,

Last night David and I got together at my house, chiefly to talk about you. The thought of you sailing somewhere in the Atlantic caused us to think of you every day. We have been feeling so distant from you over the years and as your older brothers, we believe it is our responsibility to make sure that we keep connected. Jade, we are so proud of you for following your dream. I think that what we have done is so insignificant compared to what you have undertaken. We know Mom gave you the Kiwi speech. You are the true

*Kiwi. We wish we could talk to you every
day just to tell you how much we admire
you. You are our hero. We love you.*

Love always,
David and Robert

The letter was handwritten, each brother writing every other word. "Jade, they are waiting for your call." My father handed me a piece of paper bearing David's phone number and a phone calling card. I reached for a tissue and ran to the phone. The phone conversation with David and Robert was wonderful. I covered every major event of the journey; the seasickness, my bloodied chin, the sunrises, the sunsets, the whole thing. I got updated on their families and how the wives and children were doing. All was okay in the U.K. The call lasted twenty minutes, and it was the best twenty minutes I had had with my brothers in years. I felt so connected and happy that we were part of each other's lives again. It was truly great to be a family. We made commitments to see each other when my trip was over but there was no commitment as to the location.

That night we dined with Patrick and Phil. Phil decided to stay in Salvador, as Susan was going to be flying in, as my parents did. Dinner was a detailed review of the last nineteen days. We intentionally down-played the horror of day eleven and focused on all the great days. All through the discussion my parents continued to stare at me, gaze at me, as if I were a stranger. Maybe I had changed more than I realized.

My father finally asked about the cut on my chin. So despite our intention to down-play day eleven, I was forced to give a blow-by-blow description of that miserable day at sea. I was surprised that my parents' reaction was not one of greater concern. My father simply said, "I guess you will always have your proof of your journey at sea."

"God, we think alike," I thought. Dinner went on and on, well past midnight. It was one of the best dinners and nights of my life. After dinner we said our goodbyes for the night. There were no tears, as we were looking forward to the next day.

The next three days seemed to follow a steady routine. We combined each day with sailing, shopping, dining and discussion. With Susan's arrival, Phil was distracted from his preventive maintenance responsibilities so Patrick picked up the slack. The daily schedule had me up at 7:00 a.m., followed by shower, etc., then a quick taxi ride to the hotel, breakfast with Mom and Dad, shopping in downtown, lunch, taxi to the marina, and then a nice four-hour sail on *Renovatio*. Patrick joined us sailing for each of the three days. Phil had moved off the boat to a beachfront hotel to spend private time with Susan.

Sailing *Renovatio* on the bay was delightful. The weather was made to order, and by design, Patrick did very little to help sail the boat, other than to assist with the departure and arrival at our slip. That was a multi-person job. With the use of the autopilot and electric winches, I was effectively single-handing *Renovatio*. This was important as I wanted to demonstrate to my father what I had learned and that I was capable of being out at sea in the Atlantic on a delivery assignment, especially if this was going to be a new way of life for me. With each moment that passed, my parents saw the new me; confident, fit, happy, and committed to discovery.

On the second day of our daily sails my father showed interest. He asked to operate the electric winch that was used to raise the mainsail. After an hour, he requested a seat at the helm and showed great reluctance to give it up as we approached the marina.

"Jade, when you return to Cape Town next month, maybe we should look into buying a small sailboat, something I could use in retirement, something you and I could do together."

"Sounds like a great idea." I had not told him yet that I had no intention of returning to Cape Town and this was not the time to drop the bomb on him. If I were to return, it might be in order to secure another delivery assignment.

By day three of their visit, my re-clothing was completed and I had given up the helm to my father. My mother sat in the cockpit and read her magazines on gemstones, periodically breaking into our discussion on sailing. When the conversation hit a lull I told them about my encounter with Mr. Kenney. I intentionally left out some of the details. I told them that I hoped to see him again someday but with six billion people on earth and no home or e-mail address that would be difficult. "Jade, the world is so small, have faith, some day you may be lucky." I showed my parents the sand. My mother took the packet and looked deep into it.

"All the colors of the rainbow, all the colors

of gems. Everybody needs a good luck charm. I like yours. I hope it continues to bring you good fortune." My mother then kissed the packet just as I had done and handed it back to me.

"Did Mr. Kenney say why he was in Cape Town?" my father asked.

"No, I never asked. Our conversation only lasted five minutes. He appeared and vanished so fast."

"The world is full of drifters, people who drift in and out of others' lives. They can leave great gifts behind for those they have touched. This has happened to me before and will happen to you again."

"When did you meet such a person?"

"About ten years ago, I was sitting at a restaurant in downtown having a drink. I was stressed about Robert heading off to London for school. I struck up a conversation with a young man at the bar. He told me that my concern was natural but unfounded. "Have faith in your children," he said. He mentioned something about thirteen things to remember, but I can't recall much else about the conversation. I remember thinking that he had really unusual eyes."

"Dad, that was him, that was him! Michael has one blue eye and one brown eye."

"Couldn't be. A few days later I saw a story in the local paper about a robbery in the Southend. His picture was in the article. He was murdered during the robbery."

Needless to say, I was stunned and upset. "Are you sure?"

"I'm very sure."

I turned my head toward the rail and gasped for air. Had I seen a ghost at Reubens?

By the next day, my mood had changed. It was time to say goodbye again. I promised myself it would not be a repeat of my last goodbye. I took a taxi to the hotel, met my parents for breakfast and then rode with them to the airport. The goodbye was imminent. Once the bags were checked, we walked to security. "Well this is it, Skipper," my dad said confidently. "You certainly proved yourself. You're quite a person. God, I'm going to miss you." I started to get that about to cry feeling. "Hey, no tears, come on, let's make this a happy departure. Anyway, I'll see you in two weeks and we'll have some boat shopping to do." I wasn't about to touch that one.

"Love you, Dad; love you, Mom." We hugged, kissed, and walked away. Then I turned around for one last look. They were watching me leave. They waved, blew me a kiss and walked through security.

The ride back to the marina seemed to take only minutes. Upon reflection, I was glad that the goodbye went well, but very concerned about my father's expectation for the future. Now, I needed to change my focus as Susan was also leaving and we were one day away from continuing our delivery of *Renovatio* to the BVIs.

Chapter Eleven

What a View!

We had two maintenance items left to deal with. First and most important was to resolve some problems with the autopilot and the other was to repair the wind indicator at the top of the mast. By 2:00 p.m. we were all together again on *Renovatio*. Phil went below to work on the autopilot system while Patrick and I went topside. "Well, Jade, who's going up top?" Butterflies emerged again. "Do you want to give it a shot?"

A big gulp. "Okay." I put on the boatswain's chair, loaded the tools into the right pocket, placed the new wind indicator in the left pocket and gave the thumbs up to begin the ascent.

The halyard tightened and began to pull me up the mast. The first ten feet were fine. The next ten, and the next ten brought some anxiety. "Don't look down," I thought to myself. The next twenty feet brought a rush, my heart beating like a pounding jackhammer. Then the ascent stopped. *Renovatio* rocked slightly. I gazed out. My heart relaxed. "My god, what a view," I said to myself.

"Sis, are you okay?"

"Yeah, I can't believe the view."

"Let's get the wind indicator installed." The installation only required me to unscrew one nut, remove the old wind indicator, replace it with the new one, and tighten the same nut. After that was completed, I would descend to the deck. The whole job should take no more than ten minutes.

Twenty minutes later, I was still struggling to unloosen the nut. "Too much Loctite," I yelled to Patrick. Then it moved and five minutes later the descent began.

Meanwhile, things down below were not going so well for Phil. The autopilot was failing and our ability to repair it seemed remote. "Well, I hope it holds until we arrive in the BVIs," Phil said in a worried tone. "We should have dealt with this when we first arrived here. My fault. Sorry, guys. "

"Don't worry Phil," Patrick said, not appearing to be concerned.

"Let's plan on getting underway by 6:00 a.m. tomorrow. We should be able to stay on schedule," Phil said with authority.

"So Sis, what's for breakfast?" Patrick said with a shy smile.

"Let me think about it," I said back to Patrick.

Our departure from Salvador began uneventfully. The wind from the east gave us a comfortable point-of-sail as we traveled north. The autopilot would have to do very little work under these conditions. We decided to manually steer during the day and at night if the moon lit our way. We all wanted to save the autopilot in the event we really needed it. Looking back, it was the right decision. That night the moon shone brightly on the Atlantic during my watch. "Thank God," I thought to myself. After a three-hour watch, I could get six hours sleep before I would need to get breakfast under way.

The next morning at 7:00 a.m., breakfast was ready. Phil was coming off watch and

Patrick was going on. Fresh fruit, coffee, muffins, and cereal made a great and quick breakfast. You really didn't need a chef's education to perform this task. For the next two days, and all the watches, all the meals were fine. In the last seventy-two hours we had sailed six-hundred nautical miles. We had achieved an average speed just under nine knots. On day four the weather started to deteriorate. I hoped it would be short lived. When the seas started to build, they built and built until they got to the point where I could feel fear. From two-foot swells they grew to four feet to eight feet to twelve feet, until vomiting became the norm. The six days I spent on land had hurt me. It sent me back to the beginning. Before we came into port at Salvador, I was seasoned, tested, and seaworthy. Now I felt like a rookie, all over again.

I sat in the cockpit with Patrick. Foul weather gear, tether and harness were now a part of our routine. We were unable to see ahead of us as a driving rain beat against my exposed face, each drop felt like a sewing needle prickling my skin. We debated whether to use the autopilot. We decided to engage the system. Once the "Auto" button was pushed, the system took over. That lasted five minutes. Then "Standby" displayed on the autopilot. We engaged the "Auto" button again. "Auto" flashed on, followed by the word "Standby." I tried again and the display shut down. Patrick left the cockpit to seek Phil's advice. We had a very low expectation that Phil would be able to remedy the situation. Patrick emerged. "Sis, Phil says we need to reboot the system. It's going to be tough in these conditions."

"Maybe we should wait until things settle down," I yelled over the howling wind.

"I'll give it a try." A half-hour later the system rebooted, only to shut down again. "Phil will need to look at this. I'll take the helm for now. Do you think you can get some coffee brewing?"

"Sure. Give me a few minutes."

After the coffee was made, I retreated to my cabin. I needed to get some sleep. Between the vomiting and the worrying, I was exhausted. I fell asleep quickly and began to dream. My dreaming went from good to bad instantly. My chin was cut open again but there was no blood dripping down my neck. Instead, worms oozed from my laceration. I screamed. The scream woke me. I was sweating. After fifteen minutes I fell asleep again.

This time my dreams were pleasant. I dreamt about being in a park with my nieces. We were laughing and happy. We were in Cape Town.

Several hours later I was awake again and went up to the cockpit. Phil was on watch and steering *Renovatio* through the swells. The rain had stopped. "How's the sea sickness?"

"I think I am over it," I said, while yawning.

"I think the autopilot is shot. It looks like the software is not working and the rudder reference unit has failed as well. The next few weeks are going to be tough without the autopilot."

"I know. Can I get you anything from the galley?"

"No, but thanks for asking."

By daybreak, things had settled down. The swells were now manageable and we continued to make great time as we sailed toward the Caribbean. Several days had passed and the sea decided to be kind. Being on *Renovatio* in kindly seas was a true luxury. I was half glad the autopilot failed as I now had to learn how to helm the boat in all kinds of conditions. With the sails well-balanced and the wind steady, helming took little effort; one eye on the compass, one eye on the sails, and hands on the wheel. Life was good.

Later that day I went below to my cabin and sat on the edge of my bunk. The sand was lying on my pillow. It must have fallen out of my pocket last night while I was sleeping. I picked it up and looked deep into the colors. I started to talk to Michael. "So Michael, what's next for me? Come tell me, great leader of the Bujew. Wisdom and compassion are the pathways to peace. I really need to sort out my next step. My father wants me to come home. I don't know if I can handle that. I don't want to break his heart but I don't want to break mine either. Stay the course, day by day." Then I stopped talking. I needed to get to the galley.

As the days slid by, so did my desire to think about my next move. Phil started to talk about a short stop in Trinidad with the hope of doing three things. First, was to call Susan and check on her. Second was to call the charter company in the BVIs to let them know the autopilot system needed replacement. And the last was to top off the water and fuel tanks.

Chapter Twelve

Trinidad and Beyond

Trinidad was six-hundred miles away, about a four-day sail at our current rate. We needed the sea and the wind to cooperate, and they did. The next five-hundred miles were flawless. We continued to average nine knots, and sailing *Renovatio* was as delightful as ever. The last one-hundred miles, however were quite different. The ocean became a sea of glass. The only ripples in the water were the result of flying fish skimming the surface or from our hulls sliding through the water.

Looking out the stern I concentrated on the trail we were leaving behind. It was perfectly straight. The only sound was that of our two diesel engines running at two-thousand rpm's. Then Patrick yelled out. "Whale, whale off the starboard side, aft." I spun to my left and saw one of God's magnificent creatures rise out of the sea and blow. I had seen all types of dolphins while at sea but never a whale. The whale stayed with us for hours, sometimes coming alongside and sometimes trailing behind. Every twenty minutes or so she would take a deep dive and disappear for a while, only to resurface near *Renovatio*. Finally she became bored with us, dove, showed her tail and disappeared forever. We completed the last hundred miles under power and arrived at Port of Spain, Trinidad.

After three hours, we had cleared immigration, in and out, made the necessary phone calls, refueled our two tanks, topped off the water tanks, and picked up a few provisions. Susan was doing fine, according to Phil; however, it was clear that Phil wanted to be home with her and was really longing for the end of the trip. Phil also informed us that the new autopilot system would be waiting for us in Antigua. That is where we would terminate our delivery. Another crew would be waiting to take *Renovatio* to the BVIs.

I toyed with the idea of making a few

phone calls. I still had some credit on my international calling card. Who to call -- home to my parents or U.K. to David and/or Robert? I decided to call Cape Town. The phone rang and rang only to get the answering machine.......... "Please leave a message," the machine greeting spoke.

"Mom and Dad, I am in Trinidad." The phone picked up.

"Jade, is everything okay?" It was my mother.

"Mom, hi, everything is fine. We are in Trinidad for a few hours for fuel and supplies. I wanted to let you know where I was. How's dad?"

"He's fine. Still worried about his little Kiwi. Give him a call at work if you can, and if you can't, he will understand."

"Okay, let me run. I will call you at the end of the week. Send my love to Robert and David."

"Will do. Love you, Jade."

"Love you, Mom."

I put the phone on the hook and dialed Cape Town again, only this time to Cape Town Medical Center. My father's assistant answered the phone. "Diana, this is Jade. Is my dad there?"

"Hold on, let me get him." Seconds clicked by. He picked up.

"Jade, are you okay?"

"Yes Dad, everything is fine. We made a quick stop in Trinidad and will be leaving again in a few hours. I just wanted to let you know where in the world I was."

"It sounds great to hear your voice."

"Yours too, Dad. I have been doing a lot of thinking and…"

"Jade, I know. I saw that twinkle in your eye when we sailed together a few weeks ago. I know you're not coming home to live. You must find your way in the world." My mother had gotten to him. "We will talk more about this when you're safe and sound in the BVIs."

"Thanks so much for understanding. I love you so much."

"Me, too." Silence fell over both of us, then I heard a click on the other end. His composure was gone.

"Jade, let's get a move on." It was Phil's voice this time. I jogged over to the boat feeling like the weight of the world had been lifted off my back.

The run up to Antigua from Trinidad was my least favorite part of the trip, from a wind direction point of view. Mostly, we motor-sailed into the wind. *Renovatio* doesn't like that point-of-sail. Neither do I. However, there was some good that came out of this part of the trip. It was the beautiful views of all the small islands that dot the Windward Island chain. I wanted to know these islands. I wanted to know the people. The only question was when and how.

As we traveled north, I was engrossed in reading the various cruising manuals that traveled with Phil and Patrick. Windward Islands, Leeward Islands, British Virgins, U.S. Virgins, and Spanish Virgins. There were more islands than my age. There were colonies of the Netherlands, France, Great Britain, and the U.S. There were independent nations, rich islands, poor islands, and every combination possible. I was intrigued by the now-extinct Caribbean Indians, cannibal tribes and African slaves who were brought to these islands in the seventeenth and eighteenth centuries, to exploit the natural resources, to grow sugar cane and to mine bauxite. The Caribbean, I thought, may be my new home.

Stuck in the back of my mind was a comment Patrick made, about how many people do one-way charters in the Windward Islands and that these boats have to be delivered back to the point of origin. Is this my future? Or do I use my culinary skills on a large boat and see the world, providing meals for the rich and famous? "So many possibilities," I thought. "So Michael, what is my next adventure? How about a hint?"

Phil was starting to talk about heading a bit more westerly in order to get a better point-of-sail and to conserve fuel. "Okay with me," I thought, more sailing and less motoring is a good thing. The westerly sail was a great improvement over the previous point-of-sail. I was looking forward to my watch, alone in the cockpit, hands on the wheel of *Renovatio*. I thought about Antigua and leaving our boat. I had grown to admire her builders and designers and my mates.

My interest in geography and all the classes I took over the years was truly a hint to my longing to discover the unfamiliar. My motivation was simple from the start; searching for something to love, never letting it become greedy, always being wise and compassionate, and staying true to the values bestowed upon me by my parents and the Bujew. Personal growth is a wonderful thing. It keeps you sharp and gives you a basis for confronting your fears.

Now that I knew our final destination, I began re-reading the cruising guides section on Antigua. There was so much history, so many anchorages. We were to pick up the new autopilot in Lord Nelson's Dockyard in English Harbour. This harbor had proven to be a great hurricane hole, which had saved so many boats and so many lives over the last several centuries. I was so excited to be going to such a historic place.

Another reason for my excitement was the party I had planned on attending on Shirley Heights. According to the cruising guide every Sunday night there was a party on the Heights, a hilltop with a beautiful view of both English Harbour and its neighboring Falmouth Harbour. It had been so long since I really let my hair down, as life at sea was serious business. It had been a long time since I had a drink or smoke and while I was not looking forward to a smoke, I was looking forward to a drink.

The sail past Dominica and Guadeloupe was exhilarating as the wind shifted to our advantage. These were the last two islands in the Leeward Island chain and these were two islands I wanted to explore. With so many islands of French origin I would now have the opportunity to use my four years of French classes from high school. I wished I hadn't gotten "Cs" in those classes.

Our approach to English Harbour occurred at daybreak following a short rain shower. The sunrise that morning was amazing and I took it to be a sign from above that Antigua would be good to me. At 9:30 a.m. we were tied up at Bluewater's dock. Our successful arrival was marked by Phil and Patrick each giving me a hug and a kiss on the cheek. The next order of business was a quick greeting from the Bluewater staff and then off to immigration. During the immigration process, the immigration officer asked how long I planned on staying. I told him I would be staying on *Renovatio* for a few weeks, knowing that I really had only a few days before I had to find another address.

Before the office visit, we all began to struggle with how to get home, what airline, what route, and at what price. John at Mac had a return trip allowance that we all needed to manage. For Phil and Patrick the route would be Antigua to London, London to Cape Town. Their timetable was ASAP. I, on the other hand, had no immediate business in Cape Town or anywhere else in the world. I took a different path using some of my return allowance for temporary housing and instead booked a ticket two weeks out at a much reduced fare. We all could have booked our return ticket before leaving Cape Town, but if we had, we would have had to take our departure from the BVI airport.

On Sunday morning, the day following our arrival, I walked the streets of English Harbour. Stopping by an Internet café, I e-mailed my parents and brothers. I also e-mailed John at Mac Delivery Service to see what might be available for future assignments within the Caribbean or between Cape Town and anywhere else. That afternoon I called home but there was no answer, so I left a message on the answering machine telling my parents that I had arrived in Antigua safely.

Chapter Thirteen

Shirley Heights

A few locals had told me that most people grab a cab to Shirley Heights, party, dance, and drink and then take a cab down the hill. "Sounds like a plan to me," I thought. That afternoon while *Renovatio* was getting her new autopilot I went back to the Internet café, and while having a cold drink, met several of the young people who were also working on boats. These kids were from all places from around the globe, some younger than me, some older, and mostly from Europe. Some crewed, some cleaned, some repaired, and some cooked. They told me that there was a posting board at Nelson's Dockyard primarily for the purpose of finding jobs. I decided to take a look.

Yon from Sweden and Rachel from the U.K. walked with me down to Nelson's. Then we ran into another crew member, Allison from Canada. All three of them were mid-contract, each having six to eight weeks left on their commitments. I had no weeks. Yon's job was deck hand on a catamaran called *Catmon II*. Rachel and Allison worked as wait staff on a large luxury private yacht, called *Hogwild*. *Hogwild* was owned by a meat-packer in Virginia.

We scanned the board looking for something that would fit my resume. The last posting read:

> *Chef wanted for six-month sailing assignment in the Caribbean aboard Sur Le Vent, a 251-foot schooner. Interested parties apply at Nelson's Boat Supply or e-mail T. Stoner at Stoner@surlevent.net.*

"Wow, I could do that," I said aloud.

"Go for it," Rachel said in an obvious tone.

"Yeah, it's a no-brainer."

"Maybe I will." I walked with my new friends back to the café. "By the way, are any of you going up to Shirley Heights tonight?"

"We are," said Allison and Rachel.

"I am too," replied Yon.

"Can I share a cab?"

"Sure, let's meet at the café at 5:00 p.m."

"Cool." We waved to each other and walked in different directions. I walked back to *Renovatio*.

Later that afternoon I had a chance to talk to Phil and Patrick about the chef assignment. Both of them gave me tremendous encouragement. "Jade, I'd jump on that," Patrick said.

"Sounds like a great match for you. Do it," Phil agreed.

At 5:00 p.m. I met the guys at the café and hopped a cab to the Heights. Phil and Patrick were still working on the autopilot installation and decided to forgo the party. They did think they would be in town later and I agreed to meet them at 10:00 p.m. at Nick's café for drinks, billiards and karaoke.

The ride up to Shirley Heights was not very dramatic. After a few miles of winding roads and several potholes, we arrived. I paid the four-dollar cover charge, stopped by the bar, picked up a complimentary beer, walked through a passage and then onto the hill. Then it happened. Like being hit with a wall of ice cold water on the hottest day of your life—something came over me. I was stunned, shocked, and felt a feeling so unfamiliar to me. "I am so happy to be me," I thought. "I don't ever want to be anyone else or do anything different. I want to be me and I want to be here."

Then a man, of little distinction, bumped into me, knocking my elbow. "Excuse me," he mumbled. He brought me back from my trance.

"What just happened?" I wondered.

Rachel approached me. "Are you okay?"

"Couldn't be better," I replied.

We all stood chatting and looking out at the most beautiful view of English and Falmouth Harbours. Montserrat was visible some forty miles away and I felt that if I closed my eyes and reached out I would be able to touch it.

"Hey, how about a picture?" Allison said.

"Great idea." I pulled out my digital camera and looked for a bystander to capture the moment. There in front of me was the same man who had woken me out of my trance fifteen minutes earlier. "Excuse me. Would you mind snapping a quick picture of me and my friends?"

"Be glad to. Ready, big smiles." The picture was taken. "Stay there, let me take another. Got it."

"Thanks." Then he handed the camera back to me. I flipped the switch to preview, glanced at the two pictures and looked up. He was gone. I felt a sudden panic, a familiar panic. I spun around looking in all directions but the stranger was nowhere to be found. I jumped onto a nearby rock, gaining a foot or two in height and saw the man moving through the crowd. I moved with great alacrity but once again my shortness handicapped me. Then I saw him. I approached him and tapped him on the back. He turned around.

"Excuse me, I .... ." It wasn't him. I had the wrong man. I looked all over but he was gone. Then it hit me. The voice. I knew the voice. It was Michael. No, it couldn't be. I would have noticed the eyes. This guy had brown eyes or was he wearing sunglasses?

Then I felt a tap on my arm. "Jade, are you okay? You look like you have just seen a ghost," said Allison.

"I may have." Then Yon handed me another beer and the party resumed.

Later that night I ended up at Nick's Café. The partying that began on the mountain continued well in the morning. After many beers, many games of pool and a few sorry attempts at karaoke, I left Nick's and staggered back to the boat.

The next morning I awoke with one of the worst hangovers of my life. I desperately needed a cup of black coffee and decided I was capable of making it. The first sip nearly burnt my lips so I added some cold water and continued to drink. Then I reached into my pocket. Something was wrong. Something was different. I retracted my hand. Lying in my palm was not one packet of sand, but rather, two packets. I had seen a ghost. I turned my head toward the sink and started heaving. What had happened to me on Shirley Heights?

Chapter Fourteen

The Letter

Later that day I drove Phil and Patrick to the airport using a car provided by Bluewater Charter. The journey that started more than a month ago was coming to an end. Patrick and Phil had been so important to me as I tried to discover a future for myself. And like Michael who vanished once, or maybe twice, Phil and Patrick were vanishing too. The ride to the airport started off very quietly. Patrick and Phil stared out the window as if they were looking into the darkness. Then Patrick spoke up, "Jade, you really need to pursue that job on *Sur Le Vent*. Timing is right. You are so young. Now is the time in your life to do stuff like this. Go see the world."

"Thanks for the encouragement. I'm really going to try to get that job. It should be fun. I promise I'll apply this afternoon." Then the discussion ended and silence came over us again.

As we approached the airport the discussion picked up. "Let's make sure we all stay in touch," Phil said. "I will need to send you pictures of the baby." At the departure area we exchanged e-mail addresses and phone numbers. "Look Sis, I just want to tell you one more time how much we enjoyed cruising with you. You really did a great job and I would take you on in the future for any trip."

"That goes for me too," Patrick said. All I could say was "ditto." Then the tears began to roll down my cheeks.

"Please Sis, no tears."

"Sorry. I can't help it."

"E-mail me when you get the job." They walked toward the ticketing area and I ran to the ladies room to get some tissues. I didn't realize how attached I had become to Phil and Patrick. Then I wiped my tears from my eyes and realized that for the first time in my life, I was truly alone and on my own.

On the way back to Bluewater I stopped

at Nelson's Supply and filled out an application for the chef job. Minnie from Nelson's recommended that I also e-mail Tom Stoner, the owner of *Sur Le Vent*. She also told me that no one had applied for the position since it was posted, unless they did by e-mail. Either way, I was determined to land the job. I walked to Nick's, logged on to my e-mail account, and sent a short note to Tom Stoner expressing my interest. I sorted through some other e-mails, mostly junk mail, and stared at the screen. Then a return e-mail appeared. The sender was Tom Stoner. "*Sur Le Vent* will be docked in Falmouth Harbour tomorrow. Stop by the boat for a quick interview." I replied back in the affirmative.

The next order of business was to return the car to Bluewater and find temporary housing. Ellen, a twenty-six year-old black girl, was staffing Bluewater's desk when I returned. I asked if she knew of any rooms that might be available in the area. "How long do you need a room for?"

"I hope only a week or so."

"If you want, you can crash on the couch in my apartment if it's only for a week."

"Great, how much?"

"Free for the first week."

"Great."

"By the way, I hope you're not afraid of dogs."

"No, I love animals."

"Okay. I'll be off at 6:00 p.m. My place is just a mile away. I walk to work."

"Perfect," I replied.

"By the way, I have some mail for you."

"Mail? No one has my address, how can I have mail?"

"It was lying on the floor when I opened the office this morning." She handed me a single sheet of paper folded in thirds. The letter was sealed with a single staple placed in the middle of the paper. On the outside, it read "Please forward to Jade on *Renovatio*." I became temporarily confused. "First, the second packet of sand and then this," I said to Ellen.

I decided not to read the letter until I was alone. There were a lot of places to be alone in Antigua. I walked back to *Renovatio* and sat in the cockpit. I needed to remove all of my things from the cabin as *Renovatio* would be transported to the BVIs by another crew from Bluewater. I left the letter in the galley and went down below. I stuffed the contents of my cabin into two large duffel bags and carried them to the office. Then I returned to the galley. I was afraid to open it. I didn't want to hear bad news or find out that a great opportunity had been missed. I opened the letter, first removing the staple with my fingernail. My confusion returned as I slowly opened the letter, looking toward the bottom in search of the author. The last two words read "Michael Kenney." The letter slipped from my fingertips and floated to the floor. I let it sit there awhile. I couldn't decide what emotion to feel. I was feeling everything; happiness, sadness, fear and anger. "I let him slip through my fingers," I said to myself. He was there, at Shirley Heights. How did I not recognize him? I picked up the letter. I looked at the last two words. They still read "Michael Kenney." Then I moved my eyes to the top and sat on the galley floor.

Dear Jade,

Once again we meet for only a brief moment, before some event calls us to different directions. We obviously didn't recognize each other when I took your picture the other day. You look quite different. Very fit, I might add.

Things have become very complicated for me. I would have liked to stay in An-

tigua but my boat was leaving early in the morning and I needed to start my journey back home. You see, life comes at you quickly. Sometimes you can dodge a bullet and sometimes you can't. All I can tell you is that I believe we will meet again. Where and when, I don't know, but time is of the essence. While my future is clear, yours is not. There are many things I wish to share with you but that will have to wait until our next meeting.

By the way, I slipped the sand into your pocket at Nick's last night, when you were shooting pool. I didn't want to break your concentration. And by the way, karaoke is not your thing.

I trust that the thirteen principles have treated you well. How is the Bujew? If you ever get to Hampton Roads, Virginia, look me up, and if not, have a wonderful life.

Michael Kenney

Chapter Fifteen

Sur Le Vent
(On The Wind)

I was stunned. I was angry. "Not break my concentration. What kind of an excuse is that?" I said aloud. He is like a ghost, except visible. I folded up the letter and slid it into my pocket next to the sand. I walked and walked along the streets that surrounded the harbor trying to understand why I had to live with a ghost. Why didn't he leave me his boat name or his address? The best he could do was Hampton Roads, Virginia. Where in the hell is that? How did he know about the Bujew? I thought I came up with that.

I jogged back to Bluewater Marine. "Ellen, may I use the VHF radio?"

"Sure."

I picked up the transmitter. "Michael Kenney, Michael Kenney, Michael Kenney. Bluewater Marine, Bluewater Marine." There was no reply. I tried again. Still no reply.

I jogged to the immigration office. The office was empty. I approached the immigration officer. "Excuse me. Do you think you could check your records to see if a certain person checked in or out over the last week?"

"We are not supposed to do this. Who are you looking for?"

"I'm looking for an American named Michael Kenney. He probably came in within the week." The immigration officer checked his records. There was no record of Michael Kenney.

"He must be a ghost," I said to the officer.

"Ya, must be."

That night I lay on Ellen's couch. The heat was bearable thanks to a small fan that swept the room, like a pendulum on a grandfather's clock. All night I thought about Michael. What was he doing in Cape Town two months ago? If I hadn't approached him would he have approached me? Why was he always running away? What is he hiding? I started to sound paranoid. I never fell asleep that night.

The next morning seemed to come quickly. My arms and legs felt sore, probably from carrying the two duffel bags from Bluewater to Ellen's. I left Ellen's and walked the beach and then walked into the water. It was cool and refreshing. I felt like walking until it covered my nose and mouth but stopped when the water reached my neck. I looked down at my toes. The water was crystal clear. I fell back. The water ran over my scalp and face. "Re-baptized," I thought, "by the high priest of the Bujew." I swam to shore and sat on the beach. It was time to prepare for my interview with Tom Stoner.

Later that morning I sat at Bluewater waiting to hear some indication of *Sur Le Vent's* arrival.

"*Sea Pony, Sea Pony, Sea Pony, Sur Le Vent, Sur Le Vent.*"

"Captain, this is *Sea Pony*. Please go to channel sixty-eight."

"Roger, going to sixty-eight." I followed them to sixty-eight.

"Go ahead Captain."

"I'm looking for dockage at the pier, over."

"What is your length, over."

"Length overall is two-hundred and fifty-one feet, over."

"Okay, Captain, come alongside, stern in. You will have your port side against the pier, over."

"Roger that. My ETA is eleven-hundred, over."

"Roger that, eleven-hundred."

They both signed off returning to channel sixteen. I grabbed the transmitter. "*Sur Le Vent, Sur Le Vent, Sur Le Vent*, Bluewater Marine, Bluewater Marine."

"This is *Sur Le Vent*, over."

"Go to sixty-eight."

"Roger, that, going to sixty-eight."

"Go ahead, Bluewater Marine."

"Good morning, Captain. Is there a Mr. Stoner aboard?"

"Yes, this is Tom Stoner, over."

"Mr. Stoner, this is Jade. I e-mailed you about the chef's position, over."

"Yes, how can I help you, over."

"What time would you like to meet, over?"

"How about fourteen-hundred, over."

"Confirmed, fourteen-hundred at *Sur Le Vent*."

"See you then, over." We both returned to channel sixteen.

I had three hours to get ready. A vessel of two-hundred and fifty-one feet would normally expect a level of cuisine that would exceed that of a delivery crew. I walked over to the computer and put together a quick list of proposed menu items for each meal. Each meal was broken down into three levels. There was a simple menu, a normal menu, and an elegant menu. The simple menu was for foul weather conditions and heavy seas. The normal was for everyday, and the elegant menu, should the owner wish to entertain guests or indulge himself. Crew would always eat at the simple level or normal level. I printed four copies of each and placed them in a large envelope along with my resumé and references from Smyth's Bistro. I felt very prepared.

At 2:00 p.m. I approached *Sur Le Vent*. There was an Asian man in his mid-thirties standing at the gangway holding a walkie-talkie. I requested permission to board.

"What's your business?"

"I have an appointment with Mr. Stoner. I'm interviewing for the chef position."

"If you cook as good as you look, I hope you get the job," he said, flashing me a wink. I rarely get compliments like that, I thought to myself.

"Come aboard; I'll get Tommy."

One minute later Mr. Stoner walked in, extended his hand and introduced himself. He had a hint of a British accent and was wearing a T-shirt that celebrated the victory of one British soccer team over another. He was thirty-five-ish, handsome and fit, and didn't wear a wedding ring. He had a very warm smile. For a moment I wished I was ten years older. Then we walked inside. "What a palace," I thought to myself. "I wonder what he does for a living?" We sat down.

"So Jade, tell me about your experience." I took out the information in the envelope and reviewed it with him in detail.

"Good experience; I like your approach." He reviewed the menus and reached into his pocket. "Here's two-hundred dollars. I have four guests on board. We were going to eat in town but instead, why don't you prepare dinner. If it turns out well, you've got the job. Consider it a one-meal test. Oh, by the way, I have the wine on board. Take a tour through the galley and see what you need. Deal?"

"Yes, Mr. Stoner. Deal."

"Call me Tom."

"Okay. Deal, Tom." We shook hands and

I left for the tour of the galley.

"Dinner's at 8:00 p.m.," he shouted across the saloon.

"Great, I'll be back as soon as possible. Thanks again."

The galley was well fitted out, however, the condiments and spices were in short supply. I left the galley and walked down the gang- way to the pier. When I arrived back at Bluewater Marine, I told Ellen about the interview and asked if I could borrow the car so I could drive into town to search for fresh vegetables and meat. She flipped me the car keys and thirty minutes later I walked into the market. After a quick survey of the available food, I decided on fresh asparagus salad, cold strawberry soup, steak Montreal, topped off with Gorgonzola, stuffed baked potato and stuffed tomatoes. For dessert, layers of fresh fruit and ice cream served in the champagne flute. My two-hundred dollars was spent.

I returned to the ship and started to prepare for the evening. The galley was beyond restaurant quality which made preparation easy. I solicited some help from a black housekeeper who had very little to do and wanted a free cooking lesson. After the table was set I walked out to the stern deck and met the guests. "This is Jade. She's our guest executive chef. These are friends of mine from the island."

"Nice to meet you. Dinner will be ready at 8:00 p.m."

"Great," Tommy replied. Of the four guests there was one couple, one solo guy about fifty, and a very good-looking woman, apparently Tommy's significant other. I retreated to the galley.

At 8:00 p.m. dinner began and from what I could tell, everyone really enjoyed the evening. At midnight, Tommy and Miss Perfect walked into the galley. "Jade, that was amazing. The job is yours if you want it. We sail in three days. What do you think?"

Without even asking about compensation, I replied, "I'll take it."

"Great. Come by about noon tomorrow and we'll finish up the details." Then he turned away and with his arm around Miss Perfect walked out of the galley. By the way, her name was Liz, short for Lizard. Later that night, I walked to Ellen's and collapsed on the couch. I had a new job and another new adventure. Tomorrow morning I would call home and check in with my parents, e-mail Patrick and Phil, firm up the details with

Tommy, and connect with Allison, Rachel and Yon. I had a plan.

Chapter Sixteen

Ghost Confirmed

Saturday morning came quickly. I had moved into my small bunk, which I shared with another girl who worked on board. Then I cleared immigration and said goodbye to Allison, Rachel and Yon. I was ready to start anew. Best of all, the pay was better than what I was making at Symth's. The itinerary for the next six months would take us south, island-hopping to Trinidad. Then we would sail west to the ABCs — Aruba, Bonaire and Curacao. Then sail a long leg to the Cayman Islands, Cuba, the U.S. Virgin Islands, the BVIs, and island-hop back to Antigua. I was so ready for this to start and so worried about when it would end. In the meantime, my ghost stood beside me with my thirteen principles. The Bujew.

Life on *Sur Le Vent* was good. I effectively worked an average of ten hours per day, with one and a half days off per week when the galley assistant, Juan, prepared meals off the simple menu. I also had to periodically re-provision the galley. And Liz turned out to be really nice. She appreciated the staff and treated us well. She took me out to lunch when we were in Martinique. It was fun to have some time just for "girl talk."

Each island is so different. There are different terrains, different people, different music, and different customs. Tommy had an abundance of cruising information on board which I read and re-read at every opportunity. I also started to develop a close relationship with James, one of the bridge crew. James was my age, from the U.K., educated at the North Merchants School and held no bad feelings toward South Africans. At this point I had no idea where this relationship was going but in the back of my mind I could hear Michael say, "Jade, wisdom and compassion is the pathway to inner peace."

"We are sailing to St. Martin in two days,"

James told me as we sat on the bridge.

"That's the wrong way. What about the plan to continue south?"

"The boss has some business there. Our itinerary has been changed."

"Very well, St. Martin it is."

Three days later we arrived in St. Martin and Tommy gave half of the staff the day off. He and Liz were to be gone for a few days so James and Marc, our engineer, were left in charge. We were anchored outside of Marigot. James took care of immigration for the crew and Marc took watch. Liz and Tommy had given me permission to use *Tontine*, one of the ship's inflatables.

Later that afternoon I docked *Tontine* in Anse Marcel Harbour and walked into a café for a quick drink. I was served by a Rastafarian named Reggie. He had dreadlocks down his back and was wearing a necklace fashioned with a skull that dangled from the end. I ordered an iced tea, and picked up an island entertainment magazine. After thirty minutes drifted by, I signaled for the check and paid the bill. Wanting to leave a little extra tip for Reggie, I asked him if he had change.

"Ya Mon, no problem." He reached into his pocket and pulled out a handful of bills and coins and gave me change.

Then I noticed it. "Reggie, where did you get that?"

"Get what?"

"The sand. Where did you get the sand?"

"Oh, that be the Bujew sand."

"I know what it is. Where did you get it?"

"Same place everybody get the Bujew sand."

"Where, Reggie?" I said with frustration.

"From Mr. Michael."

"What do you know about him?"

"Mr. Michael, he help many people on the island after the big hurricane. He preaches compassion. Everybody know Mr. Michael."

"Do you know how to contact him?"

"He lives in Baginia, mon. Wherever dat is? He be back when the next disaster hits. He always come back."

"How long have you had the sand?"

"Forever, mon. It come from my father just before he died. That was ten years ago." I was dumbfounded. "Mr. Michael have special power. Bujew power." He walked away shaking his head. I walked back to *Tontine* and reached into my pocket. Two packets accounted for. I returned to *Sur Le Vent* in a daze.

Chapter Seventeen

James

The days following our departure from St. Martin were very important days as I continued to expand my self-awareness. Before I left Cape Town I had felt that love was all about love for something, rather than love for someone. That belief was starting to change.

We anchored *Sur Le Vent* just off Gustavia Harbour in St. Barts. St. Barts is so different from the other Caribbean islands. Because of its terrain and lack of annual rainfall, the island was never exploited. There was nothing to mine, no sugar cane to grow, no slaves to import. St. Barts is French, white, and does not have the Third World feeling that so many other islands possess. The island has great restaurants, cafés, jazz bars, beautiful homes, and beautiful beaches. As such, it is the home of the very rich and the stopping point for very large yachts from around the world.

On the morning of our second day in Gustavia, James and I went ashore. It was our day off. To this point our relationship focused on friendship but I could feel our friendship changing. We tied the dinghy at the dinghy dock and began to walk along the streets of Gustavia. Then like a scene from a movie, our hands touched, then our hands locked. At that moment we were no longer just friends. We stopped at a café on one of the side streets, ordered breakfast, and looked out at the people walking by. The morning sun had cast long shadows over the street and for a moment I fantasized about being an artist or a photographer with the skills to capture the scene.

After breakfast we walked along the harbor looking at all the boats that were moored beside each other. Most were small boats. One caught our eye. She was a thirty-six foot custom sloop, beautifully maintained and flying a French flag. Her name was *Entre*

Nous (Between Us.) James stood behind me, his hands around my waist. "What a beautiful boat. All it needs is for you and I to be together on her to sail the world." His lips touched my neck. A wonderful feeling came over me. "Jade, I think I'm falling in love with you."

I was speechless for a moment. "Me too," I said, knowing I meant it. I turned around toward him. We embraced and kissed. I was falling in love.

All morning long we walked the streets of Gustavia talking about our immediate future. Later that afternoon we took a cab to Bikini Beach, rented a Sunfish and sailed along the coast. We took turns with the rudder as the other trimmed the sails. We were equal in skill and equal in our developing love for each other. That night we dined in Gustavia at Edward's Bistro. I felt so grown up and mature, like a woman with a husband who had seen the world. We shared a bottle of wine, had a delicious dinner and continued our discussion about our future. After dinner we walked down to The Buzz, a jazz bar on the inner harbor. K. J. Denhert, an urban jazz musician/singer from New York played her unique style. It was an earthy sound that really appealed to me. We bought two of her CDs, walked back to the dinghy and returned to *Sur Le Vent*.

Several days later we anchored in Charlestown, Nevis. James and another crew member had gone ashore to deal with customs. The process seemed to take a very long time. He was gone for four hours. I began to worry. Worrying about a man other than my father was foreign to me.

Tom and Liz were entertaining some insurance executives on board, so the demand on my time was extensive. Liz had some special requests that didn't challenge my skills but did challenge my inventory. All day long I worked in the galley getting ready for the festivities. At day's end, James appeared in the galley. "How's my favorite chef?"

"Tired. I have been on my feet all day. Dinner will begin at 7:00 p.m. and probably go to midnight."

"I have the bridge tonight. Meet me there after you get off. I have a surprise for you." My tiredness vanished.

At 7:00 p.m., Tom and two crew members went ashore to retrieve his guests. The six couples were staying at the Four Seasons Resort. The six men were members of an insurance syndicate that insured *Sur Le Vent*. They were Brits, each one more charming than the next. All night long, course after course, they raved about the dinner and service. After dessert, I was summoned to the dining room. As I walked in, the seven couples stood and applauded. They raised their glasses. "Our compliments to the chef," rang out in unison.

"Bloody good show," said one of the guests.

"Jade, great job," said Liz.

At 2:00 a.m. I left the galley. I had assigned breakfast responsibility to Juan, my galley assistant. I walked to the bridge. Taking watch at anchor is a matter of monitoring the various systems that run the vessel. James was sitting at the controls as I walked in. "How did dinner go?" he said as he approached me.

"It was a total success." He kissed me, reached into his back pocket and pulled out a rectangular box.

"I picked this up in town earlier today. Open it." For a moment it felt like Christmas. I unwrapped the box and opened it. Inside was a gold pendant and chain. The pendant was in the shape of a whale's tail and had a ruby in the center. I turned around, he placed it on my neck and closed the clasp.

"James, I love it. It's perfect." I kissed him.

"I wanted to get something for a very special lady." We kissed again. Then Kevin walked in.

"James, you're off, I'm on."

"Thanks, mate." We left the bridge, walked to James's cabin and made love.

Chapter Eighteen

The Third Meeting

For the next four months, life aboard *Sur Le Vent* was like a case study on how to enjoy life. Everything in Cape Town was fine. My father had given six months' notice to Cape Town Medical Center and was so excited about his retirement. Robert and David, the sisters-in-law, and the kids were doing fine in England. My mother was buying and selling more gems than ever, and James and I were deeply in love. We planned to visit his family in the U.K. at the end of our assignment. My parents were considering flying to London to see the grandchildren while I was there. The plan, if executed, would be the best family reunion a girl from Cape Town could ask for. The only thing not yet resolved was my next meeting with Michael.

Thirty days later our luck changed. *Sur Le Vent* had two major failures in its systems. First, the hydraulic system for the rudder started to have intermittent problems and then the refrigeration system that provided the heating and cooling failed. Tommy made arrangements to bring the boat to Fort Lauderdale for repair but the yard he usually used could not accommodate him. They recommended that we take *Sur Le Vent* to Norfolk, Virginia, for the needed repairs. When the news spread of our change, I went to the communication room and logged onto the computer. I searched the web for Norfolk. I was linked to HR.com. HR was the abbreviation for Hampton Roads. I retrieved the letter from Michael and read the last line.

If you ever get to Hampton Roads, Virginia, look me up, and if not, have a wonderful life.

"I can't believe this. I'm going to find him if it kills me," I said aloud.

Two weeks later we limped into Norfolk, Virginia, motored down the Elizabeth River and turned our ship over to Sun Engineering.

Sur Le Vent would be out of commission for thirty days. We were allowed to stay aboard during the time repairs were made. My galley duty was off the simple menu, so I had a lot of time on my hands.

The second day of our stay it rained so I spent most of my time on the Internet looking for Michael. All the name searches failed. Bujew failed. Then I had a hit. The search for "mandala" and "Hampton Roads" linked me to a newspaper article about Tibetan monks creating a mandala sand painting in Hampton, Virginia. I MapQuested the location. The monks would be in town next week. My luck was improving and I began to feel as if I was going to confront my ghost.

The next five days clicked by. James and the engineering staff worked alongside the repair crew from Sun. Tommy and Liz were gone most of the time. My assistant was handling the galley, and I was renting a car for the short drive to Hampton. At 4:00 p.m. I arrived at the small auditorium in the village of Phoebus, part of the city of Hampton. I was so nervous. I expected to walk in and see Michael standing there, waiting for me, unable to vanish. I could hear the monks chanting. I could smell incense burning. The scent was delightful. My skin was full of goose bumps. There were thirty or so people milling around, looking at the monks work their magic with the sacred sand. The colors were vibrant, almost shocking. I approached the monks and watched them work and pray. I saw the very origin of my sand emerge. Then it hit me. Michael said it came from a friend named Curry. I left the monks and walked back to the lobby.

There was a man in his fifties, wearing beads on his wrists and neck and talking to two monks. Our eyes met and locked on each other. He approached me. "Excuse me, I'm looking for Michael Kenney or a person named Curry. Do you know either of them?" He stared deep into my eyes, almost creating panic within me.

"I'm Paul Curry. You must be Jade." My knees started to feel weak. "I suppose you are here to see Michael."

"Yes, do you know where he is?"

"Yes, I see him every day. I will take you to him, but first I must get something from my office. Stay right here." He walked up a flight of stairs. I waited anxiously, wondering what he was doing. Then he walked down and signaled me to follow him. We walked out a side door, down an alley and onto the street.

"He is just around the corner. So, how has the sand treated you, Jade of South Africa?" I looked up at him. He was very tall. "Here we are," his mood changing to sadness.

"Where? He lives in a church?"

"No, he lives over there." Paul's arm was extended, his fingers pointing specifically to a large stone in the church's cemetery. "This is Michael Kenney's new home. He died two weeks ago." I started to collapse. Paul's large hands grabbed me under my arm to steady me. Tears poured down my face. I felt as empty as I ever felt in my life. I was lifeless. A part of me was dying.

"Jade." The voice startled me. "Walk with me." We walked, my knees shaking. We stopped in front of the stone. It read Michael Kenney. There was no birth date or death date. The stone looked to be hundreds of years old. It had been used before, by others who had died and been buried at this church. I tried to make out other names but the engravings had been filled in with mortar. I wondered if Michael had been buried here before.

Then Paul helped me down to my knees. The sun on my face felt warm. All the noise around me had stopped except for the sound of birds nesting in a nearby tree.

His hand touched my shoulder. I looked up. "This is for you." He handed me a letter, one page folded in thirds, and sealed by a single staple. "I have been holding this for you. Michael knew you'd be coming someday. He told me he didn't know when but he was sure that you would be coming." Paul walked away. I sat there crying as anyone would, who had lost a very close friend. I opened the letter. It was hard to read through my tears.

Dear Jade,

So we missed each other this time. My loss.

The sand you have carried is a reminder of life's impermanence. The monks create a mandala in honor of life and prayer and shortly thereafter destroy it, to demonstrate life's fragility. We Buddhists do not fear death. Death is a part of life. We are all reincarnated over and over again. It's a circle, not too different from the circle you and I have created. I found you in Cape Town and now you have found me. Continue your dreams, and your adventure. Someday you will fall in love. You will have children and you will return to Cape Town.

Everything that has occurred in this life has been for the sole purpose of our final meeting. The day I met your father many years ago, and our two meetings, are all part of a much larger plan. While all of this may be very confusing to you, someday it will make perfect sense as we will learn to love each other in ways you cannot imagine. This is our destiny.

Have wonderful life, Jade, of South Africa.

Sincerely,
Michael Kenney.

I looked back at Curry. He nodded. I looked back at the stone and reached into my pocket. I took out one packet of sand and held it in my hand. "Goodbye, Michael. Thanks for all you have done." The package fell from my hand, the seal breaking. Then the sand separated from the packet and rained over his grave.

Chapter Nineteen

In the End

I drove back to Sun Engineering in a fugue state. I have no recollection of how I got from the auditorium to *Sur Le Vent*. I was troubled by the discussion my father and I had in Brazil regarding the death of Michael Kenney. I went to the communications room and logged on to the Internet. My first e-mail was to the newspaper in Cape Town. I explained the situation in detail and requested that the newspaper research my issue. A quick e-mail was returned, indicating that they would do so and that I would hear back in two days. Two days later I received an e-mail from D. Ross from the "corrections desk." She explained that there was a mix-up in the newspaper.

Michael had been in town to give a lecture on "Religious Convergence." There was an ad in the paper featuring the seminar. The ad included his picture and his name. On the opposite page was the story of the random killing in Cape Town, the story my father read. The victim's name was Mitchell Kearney. The newspaper mistakenly put Michael Kenney's name and picture in the murder story and Mitchell Kearney's name and picture in the seminar ad. Two days following the story, the newspaper printed a retraction and apology. My father did not notice the correction. I forwarded the e-mails to my father. Case closed.

Everything Michael said in his letter came true. Over the next five years James and I continued our adventure. We visited ports throughout the world and took assignments on various ships. We spent time on *Leander*, one of the most luxurious motor yachts afloat. We even did a six-month tour on *Hogwild*, the boat Rachel and Allison crewed on. But in the end we kept coming back to *Sur Le Vent*.

Tommy and Liz had gotten married two years earlier and Liz was pregnant with twins. Neither Phil nor Patrick delivered boats anymore but they still worked at Mac. Phil was managing the marina and Patrick worked in the brokerage operation. Each had one son and Donna and Susan loved motherhood.

Over the years we had made many trips to the U.K. to visit James's family, always staying in their country home just outside Arundel. I had grown very close to his parents and felt very much at home in England. We had thought about making it our permanent home but the weather and the short sailing season kept us in the lower latitudes.

Last year, Tommy and Liz invited our family for a 10-day cruise on *Sur Le Vent*. At the time, she was sailing in the Mediterranean. James and his parents, my brothers, and their families flew from England to Nice, France, to meet us. My parents flew in from Cape Town.

Two days into the cruise, James and I stood with our families on the bow of *Sur Le Vent*, exchanged vows and were wed. The wedding ceremony was beautiful. Our rings were selected by my mother, the gem expert, and the readings were a mixture of Bujew. My wedding dress was simple. James wore dress whites. In his breast pocket was our sand. The rest of the cruise was wonderful. Each day was like a day in paradise. Our families fell in love with each other as James and I had and I felt as if life going forward was going to be wonderful.

A few months after the wedding we returned to Cape Town to work at Mac Delivery Service. The company was under new ownership; the new owners were James and Jade Morison.

At the end of "B" dock, there is a twenty-four foot Timberpoint daysailer. She is a beautiful wooden boat that I acquired on the Internet and had shipped to Cape Town. She was built in the 1930s in Greenport, New York, and was refurbished at Mac. This is my father's boat. This is the boat that we sail together. Her name is *Gem*. Her refit was paid for by my mother.

On December tenth, I gave birth to a little baby girl. We decided to follow my mother's naming convention. Her name is Ruby M. You know what the "M" stands for. The baby looks a little bit like James and a lot like me, with one exception. She has one blue eye and one brown eye.

Afterword

An Author's Confession

It had been seven years since I completed my second book. The first two books were inspirational autobiographies. I had given up writing because I had not found anything to write about. However, in January 2007, I met someone who inspired me to write again.

I was on top of Shirley Heights, in Antigua, when we met. We spoke for ten minutes. She was twenty-six years old and from South Africa. She worked as a crew chef on a private luxury yacht owned by a European celebrity. Her mother was from New Zealand and sailed as a child. She had a brother who lived in the U.K. Some time after completing cookery school, she joined a delivery crew for a major boat manufacturer, and delivered a forty-six foot catamaran from South Africa to a charter base in Europe. Her name started with a "J". That's all I knew.

I left Shirley Heights regretting that I didn't get her name and e-mail address. Her story could have been my third book. Instead, I decided to write this story, loosely based on the facts that I gathered that day.

Truth be known, this book is also about me. When I arrived on Shirley Heights that day, I did not get the feeling that Jade had gotten. That day and at that moment, what ran through my head was that I was so tired of being me. And like Jade, the feeling and the trance only lasted five minutes or so. It was one of the friends, with whom I was sailing, who bumped my arm and jolted me back to reality.

I played two other characters in the book. I was Jade's father. I am a middle-aged baldheaded, healthcare executive, who has been focused on retirement. And I am Michael Kenny. I am a member of the Bujew faith. Bujews are people who have found meaning, in the merger of Judaism and Buddhism. Judaism encourages people to look to God for answers. Buddhists encourage people to look within themselves for answers. The faiths are complementary. Bujew is also a word used to describe married couples, where one member is Jewish and one member is Buddhist. There are also Hinjews, where one member of a married couple is Hindu and the other Jewish. If you're so inclined to search the Web, you'll find many sites regarding Bujewism.

In 2001, I attended an educational seminar at the American Theater, in Hampton, Virginia. The Tibetan monks were in residency, lecturing about Tibetan Buddhism and the Dalai Lama. The monks were also creating the wisdom mandala. As in the book, the mandala was destroyed at the end of its completion. The director of the American Theater, Michael Paul Curry, a very close friend of mine, gave me a packet of sand from the wisdom mandala. I have carried that sand with me in my wallet since that day.

Many other characters in the book are real people who I know or who I love. The "whale" story line happened to me during my 2006 cruise in the Caribbean. Most of the islands visited by Jade have been places I have sailed. I have either dined or drank in all the restaurants visited by Jade. And James was a takeoff of a young second officer I met on a cruise in the Aegean Sea in 2007. The autobiographical references go on and on.

After the completion of the book I was able to find some additional information about the young woman who inspired me. I have made several attempts to e-mail her in the hopes of getting some firsthand knowledge of her adventure so I could incorporate her actual voyage into the book. At this point I have not heard from her. So, Jade, if you would ever like to coauthor a book about your adventure, search the Internet and find me.

One Last Note: In the final stages of production of this book, Jade did contact me. She remembered our meeting at Shirley Heights and we agreed to remain in touch about future writing projects.

Glossary

Aft: *behind the boat or toward the stern.*

Bow: *the forward end of the boat.*

Bonine: *seasickness medicine.*

Fall Off: *to steer the boat away from the direction of the wind.*

Hull: *the main body of the boat.*

Jib or Headsail: *the forward sail.*

Loctite: *a red liquid that is applied to a nut and bolt, which stops the nut from loosening.*

Luff: *when sailing close to the oncoming wind, the front of the sail trembles or shakes. The luff is removed by either trimming the sail or by steering the boat away from the direction of the wind.*

Main or Mainsail: *the sail that is attached to the mast on a single mast boat.*

Point-of-sail: *direction of the boat in relation to the wind.*

Port: *the left side of the boat, looking toward the bow.*

Reef: *to reduce the amount of sail area that is exposed to the wind.*

Starboard: *the right side of the boat, looking toward the bow.*

Stern: *the rear end of the boat.*

Thru-hull: *a fitting that goes through the hull of the boat.*

Trim: *to set a sail in correct relation to the wind by tightening or loosening a line.*